# MONTANA LIGHTS AND MISTLETOE NIGHTS

## A KINGS OF RETRIBUTION MC CHRISTMAS

SANDY ALVAREZ

CRYSTAL DANIELS

TWO PENS-

CRYSTAL Daniels

Sandy ALVAREZ

-ONE STORY

# 1

## GABRIEL

Like most mornings, I lie awake and stare at my woman. Wisps of her blonde hair flutter across her parted lips with every exhale of breath. A sense of peace settles over me while I continue to watch her sleep. There was a time in my life I didn't want any of this: marriage, home, a family. Alba was—is—my salvation. She has given me a life I never thought possible for a man like me. Now, we have a home filled with love and two beautiful children.

*Alba is and always will be the light to my dark.*

I reach out and rest my palm against her swollen belly. My woman is pregnant with our third child. I feel the baby kick against my palm and wonder how my Alba can sleep through it. My eyes leave her face and trail over her breasts, barely contained in the silk baby-blue nightgown she's wearing.

Her eyes open. "Hi," she rasps in a sleep-filled voice.

"You are so beautiful, Cariño." My hand slides down her leg. Alba's body responds, and her legs part. I kiss my way down her inner thighs as I settle between them. My touch causes her to shiver. Grabbing both of her hips, I pull her closer and taste her sweet pussy. She bucks against my tongue.

Fisting my hair, Alba moans, "Gabriel." I swipe my tongue through her wet pussy again, making her gasp.

"You taste so fuckin' good." I manipulate her swollen clit while sliding two fingers inside.

"God, yes," Alba pants.

"Whose pussy is this?" I continue my assault on her bundle of nerves.

Her nails drag across the top of my scalp. "Yours. Always yours." She gasps again. "I'm going to come."

I take one last taste before rising. Alba peels her nightgown over her head, tossing it to the floor. Her eyes lower to my cock. "I need you inside me."

"On your side." I settle in beside her and grab hold of her thigh, bringing her leg back to rest over my hip. I place the head of my cock at her entrance, then slowly sink into her. "Fuck," I hiss when her walls tighten. Alba's hips rock back, matching my rhythm.

"Gabriel," Alba moans, and I know she's close.

"Come, Cariño." And she does. Her pussy strangles my cock so hard flashes of light dance behind my eyelids. "Fuck!" I roar as my release explodes right along with hers.


A short time later, the four of us gather in the kitchen. Gabe tugs at Alba's sweater as she fixes his breakfast. "Mommy, Val is hungry."

"I know, baby. I'll feed her when I finish fixing your eggs." Alba stirs them in the skillet, then sprinkles cheese over the top. Gabe strolls back to where his sister sits in her high chair, happily playing with a light-up toy that plays Christmas music, which Bella bought for her last week.

"So, what's on your agenda today?" Alba asks, setting Gabe's plate in front of him. Alba stretches and rubs her back.

I stand. "Sit." I point to her chair at the table and start fixing her plate of food. Alba doesn't argue. She takes her seat and begins tending to Val. "I have a back piece today."

"Yeah? Anyone, I know?" Alba asks, trying to get our daughter to pay less attention to the toy and eat.

"Grimshaw." I sit Alba's plate of food in front of her.

"Isn't he the guy who built that massive house on the lake just down from Nikolai and Leah's place?"

"That's him." I pour myself a cup of coffee. "Want something to drink?" I ask Alba.

"Hot chocolate sounds good." I hear the smile in her voice.

"Me too?" Gabe asks.

"Finish your eggs first," Alba tells him. I mix a cup of hot chocolate, along with an extra cup for our son, and take them to the table before sitting down with my food and drink. "I hear he's loaded—as in millions." Alba pops a bite of bacon into her mouth. "I wonder what he does for a living."

"He plays football." I quench her curiosity.

"Pro?"

"Yeah, babe. He's the star quarterback for his team."

About an hour later, it's time for me to head out. Before heading into the garage, I grab my coat hanging from the hook on the laundry room wall and slide it over my cut. "Daddy, Daddy!" Gabe shouts. I hear the thudding of shoes smacking against the wood floor. Gabe enters the laundry room wearing a pair of my black leather boots, their tops stopping at his knees. My lip twitches in amusement.

"Come here." I pluck him from the floor, and my boots remain where he once stood. "Take care of your momma and baby sister while I'm away, yeah?"

Gabe crosses his arms across his chest. "Okay," he says with a serious tone.

"You be good today, and I'll bring home some candy," I whisper, trying not to let Alba hear.

Alba appears holding Val, and Gabe says, "I get candy if I'm good."

Alba raises her brow and eyes me. "Says who?"

Gabe does his best chest puff. "My daddy, and he's the boss."

I do my best to stifle a chuckle and clear my throat. "He said it, not me." Alba shakes her head wearing a smile, but says nothing as our eyes stay locked on one another. Val squirms in Alba's arms, reaching for me. "The weather report said we would get more snow today and a possible snowstorm next week. I'll have to make a run to the store and stock up on supplies just in case we get snowed in."

"Send me a list, and I'll stop on my way home." I kiss Gabe on top of the head and lower him to the floor. He immediately slides his little legs back into my boots, then runs out of the laundry room. Alba passes our daughter to me. Val lays her head against my chest. She's so sweet and loving, just like her momma. "You should be takin' it easy. And I don't want you traveling alone so close to your due date." I look at my wife.

"Stop worrying so much. I'll be fine. Besides, I'm doing a little Christmas shopping with the girls today, too, so I won't be alone." Alba moves closer, her feet shuffling against the floor. She tugs on my beard, bringing my face to hers. "I love you, you know." I feel her lips lift in a smile as they brush against mine.

"Don't overdo it today."

Her breath smells like chocolate from the hot cocoa she previously drank. "You're so bossy," she whispers as she keeps running her fingers through my beard.

"You love it," I say, and Alba's pupils dilate. "And you rub my beard one more time, I'm throwin' you over my shoulder and we're gettin' naked," I growl. "I love you, Cariño." I kiss her.

As I back my truck out of the driveway, it begins snowing, adding to the few inches already blanketing the ground. Before putting the vehicle in drive, I glance back at the house and catch Gabe's little face squished against the glass of the living room window. He does this every morning as I head out, and he's always there watching for me when I return. I give him a nod, then pull away from the house.

The drive into town is short. I park my ride in front of the club's tattoo shop, Kings Ink, and climb out. I unlock the front door, step inside, and turn on the lights. I look around, happy with the updated décor. Grey, along with Adira, our new tattoo artist, took my ideas and brought everything together. The walls are painted a deep royal purple with framed tattoo art paintings, displayed like gallery pieces. I pass the small waiting area, where black leather furniture sits atop a gray area rug as I make my way toward the back of the shop.

I glance at the clock on the wall. My first appointment with Hawken Grimshaw is within the hour, so I sit down at my workstation and inventory what I'll need for his session.

The rush of cold air from the front door opening causes me to look up. Grey strides inside, holding a box from Grace's bakery. Adira is right behind him, carrying four coffees. "How's it goin', boss?" Grey strides across the room to the snack area and sits the box beside the coffee machine. My only response is a grunt. "I'll take that as a positive start to our Friday." He opens the bakery box and plucks out a candy cane-shaped cherry Danish.

Adira brings me a coffee. "Here." She sits it off to the side, away from my equipment. "An apology for not being here to open this morning and have coffee already made."

Adira was hired almost a year ago and has proven to be a great fucking artist.

I glance at Adira. She looks exhausted. "How's your sister?"

There is a lot of emotion in her eyes when I inquire about Mya. Adira's older sister has ovarian cancer. She's been battling it for a long time, but now her cancer has become resistant to treatment.

"Mya is having a good morning." Adira smiles, but it doesn't reach her eyes. "So—" She walks to her station. "How's Alba and the kiddos?" She steers the conversation away from her.

"Good."

For the next several minutes, the three of us keep to ourselves, setting up for our first tat sessions of the day. The front door chimes and another blast of cold air wafts in, along with Grimshaw. "How's it going?" Grey gives him a chin lift.

Grimshaw pulls the knit hat from his head and shrugs off his winter jacket. He hangs them on the coat rack by the door. "I'm good, man." He shakes Grey's hand.

"I'm ready for you, brother," I call to him, and he makes his way toward me.

Grimshaw's steps slow on his way past her station, where she's bent over digging through a supply drawer. His eyes plaster on her ass.

"You staring at my ass, Grimshaw?"

"I am." Grimshaw doesn't even attempt to lie. Adira straightens and faces him.

"You're a pig." Adira folds her arms across her chest.

"You asked, sweetheart." Grimshaw stands there a beat before walking away.

"Lose the shirt," I tell him, and he strips it over his head, tossing it to the empty chair a few feet away. Behind him, I catch Adira's attention fixed on my client. The moment Grimshaw turns, she quickly spins around. He sits, straddling the chair. Usually, I wouldn't say shit, but I like Adira and feel a brotherly protectiveness. "She's going through some shit." I grab the bottle of green soap and cleanse his back. "If your only intention is to get her in the sack, then don't fuck with her. You got me?" I keep my voice low but my tone hard enough to make my warning understood.

Grimshaw glances across the room at Adira and nods. "Message received."

2

———

# ALBA

"Are you going to be good and help Miss Emma with your sister today?"

Gabe looks up at me from his spot on the living room floor where he's playing with his toy motorcycle and nods. Walking over to him, I crouch down and run my fingers through his black hair. "How about I bring home that movie you've been wanting to see? We can watch it tonight, and I'll have Papi bring pizza home."

"Yeah!" Gabe's face lights up.

"Deal." I kiss his cheek.

A moment later, the doorbell rings. Standing, I make my way over to the door. Peering through the window, I see Emma standing there. After punching in the code to the alarm, I pull open the door and smile. "Hi."

Emma gives me a smile of her own. "Hey."

Stepping aside, I let her in. "Thank you so much for coming out to watch the kids."

Emma waves her hand. "It's no problem. I have the day off, and I would rather be doing something to keep busy rather than sitting alone in my apartment all day. Besides, your kids are great. I love them. They never give me a lick of trouble."

I beam at her compliment of my children. "They love you too." Turning, I walk into the kitchen and grab my purse off the kitchen table. "Val is asleep upstairs. She's been down for about thirty minutes, so you should have another solid hour before she wakes up. And Gabe is playing in the living room." Just as I turn back to face Emma, I hear a car horn. "That would be Bella. Call me if you need anything."

"Don't worry about us. We'll be fine," Emma tells me.

I poke my head around the corner of the living room. "Bye, buddy. Mommy will see you later. Love you."

"Bye, Momma." Gabe waves.

I wait until I hear the locks click in place and for Emma to set the alarm before I carefully make my way down the front steps toward Bella's car. Luckily, Gabriel makes sure to keep the ice and snow off the porch so that I don't slip and fall.

"Come on, preggers!" Bella hollers out the car window. "Waddle a little faster."

"I'm coming!" I shout back. "Keep your pants on."

"Somebody needs to keep their pants on, and it isn't me." My sister giggles when I open the passenger door.

Tossing my purse into the back seat, I shoot her a glare. "Funny," I deadpan.

"I thought so." My sister smirks.

"Would you stop rushing me? I'm moving as fast as I can." I plop down in the seat and shut the door.

"We only have a couple of hours before we meet the girls at Charley's, and that doesn't leave us much time to shop." Bella puts the car in gear before maneuvering out of the driveway.

"I don't know why you insist on decorating the clubhouse every Christmas. You know the guys are just going to throw a fit. They do every year," I tell her.

"I know." Bella giggles. "That's what makes it so fun."

"You're terrible." I shake my head and grin.

"Hey, I have to get my kicks from somewhere. Why not do it by giving the guys a hard time?"

Bella and I spend the next two hours picking out lights, artificial trees, ornaments, and garland. She even insisted on a twenty-foot blow-up Santa. Now we are on our way to the clubhouse to drop the stuff off before heading to Charley's. "Can you go faster? I have to pee."

"You just went to the bathroom before we left the store," Bella laughs.

"I have Gabriel's mammoth-sized spawn doing cartwheels on my bladder. I can't help it."

"Yeah, and it has nothing to do with that super-sized iced tea you finished chugging a few minutes ago," Bella mutters.

Ignoring her, I reach into the back seat, grab some chips from one of the shopping bags and regard my sister. "I have a feeling Santa is going to meet the same demise as Frosty from last Christmas."

Bella rolls her eyes. "Probably, but it's still worth all this effort. As I said, it's my own brand of personal entertainment."

By the time we roll up to the clubhouse, my bladder is about to burst. Charging through the door, I spot a few guys, including Gabriel, sitting around but don't stop to socialize.

"Hey there, darlin'." Quinn appears from down the hall. "What's the hurry?"

I nearly knock him over when I shove him out of my way. "Can't talk. Need to pee."

As I'm making a beeline for the bathroom, I hear Logan's voice ring out from the main room of the clubhouse. "Angel, I thought we talked about this. No more Christmas shit at the clubhouse."

. . .

After finishing my business, I open the bathroom door to find Gabriel leaning up against the wall in the hallway. My steps falter when I take in his tall form. To this day, the sight of him still makes my tummy flutter. "Hi. I thought you had a client today. The football guy."

"Lunch break" is all Gabriel says as he pushes off the wall. And like a lion stalking its prey, he marches toward me. Once I'm within arm's reach, he snakes his arm around my waist and backs me up into the bathroom before kicking the door shut with his booted foot.

A second later, we start going at it. Gabriel's mouth is on mine, and my hands frantically tear at his t-shirt. A growl erupts from his chest when my nails rake down his chest, leaving my mark. I just had Gabriel inside me this morning, but I can't get enough of him. I would blame pregnancy hormones, but it's not... It's him.

"I need to be buried inside your pussy," Gabriel grunts.

I kiss along the column of his neck and shiver.

"Turn around and put your hands on the counter, Cariño."

Not wasting any time, I do as he says. The moment I turn, Gabriel shoves my jeans down, taking my panties with them. My sex clenches at the sound of him releasing his belt buckle. A whimper escapes past my lips when the blunt head of his cock teases the seam of my pussy.

"Always wet for me."

"Always," I pant.

Gripping my hips in his large hands, Gabriel drives forward, burying himself deep inside me. Closing my eyes, I throw my head back and scream. "Oh, god!"

"Eyes forward," he growls.

When I peel my eyes open, I'm met by his dark, intense stare through the reflection of the mirror. A snarl escapes past his lips with each thrust he delivers. Like a wild force, Gabriel consumes my body. Just like he does every single time he's inside me.

Releasing my hips, two large, tattooed hands make their way above my head as Gabriel braces his palms flat against the mirror in front of me the same time his chest settles over my back, his closeness allows him to sink deeper inside of me, and I choke on a gasp. "Gabriel."

"Come for me, Cariño," he demands. And my body does just that. The moment Gabriel buries his face into the crook of my neck, biting the sensitive flesh, I come with white flashes of light bursting behind my eyelids, taking him with me.

Neither one of us moves for several seconds until there is a knock at the door.

"Hey," Bella calls out. "If you two are done boning, we need to get a move on. The girls are waiting."

I huff out a laugh and shake my head. *I'm going to kill my sister.*

My breath hitches at the loss of Gabriel when he pulls out of me. Then with the kind of tenderness that makes my heart melt, he tugs my jeans back in place, stopping briefly to kiss my round belly. Once we both have our clothes back in place, we exit the bathroom and make our way back up front, where Bella is waiting with the guys.

"Finally!" She hops down from the stool at the bar. My face turns a lovely shade of red when Quinn turns a knowing smirk in mine and Gabriel's direction. He opens his mouth to let word vomit spill, but Gabriel stops him.

"Shut the fuck up."

Quinn chuckles. "I didn't say anythin', brother."

"No, but your ass was about to," Logan interjects before turning his attention to my sister, slapping her ass. "You women behave."

Bella winks at Logan. "Don't we always?"

Logan tosses his head back and barks out a laugh. "No."

"Whatever," my sister huffs, tossing her purse over her shoulder. "Come on, Alba."

Turning back toward Gabriel, I thread my fingers through his beard and pull him down toward my mouth, sealing my lips over his. "I'll see you later."

"Bye, baby."

Fifteen minutes later, Bella and I walk into Charley's, and from the looks of it, we are the last to arrive. Our girls are at the back of the bar, where three tables are shoved together.

"Ladies." Charley smiles and tips his head.

I give him a wave. "Hi, Charley."

When we walk up to the group, Glory is the first to greet us. "It's about damn time. I'm already on my second margarita."

"It wasn't my fault this time, ladies." Bella hooks a thumb over her shoulder toward me. "This one was boning her man in the bathroom at the clubhouse."

"Bella!" I slap my sister on the arm, and my face heats from embarrassment.

"Now that," Glory says, lifting her glass in the air and winking at me, "is an excuse I can accept. A good dicking is the only good excuse there is for being late for your girls. And by the glowy look on your face, I'd say it was good."

"That's pregnancy glow," Leyna interjects.

Glory shakes her head. "Nope. There is pregnancy glow, and there is good dick glow, and Alba's is the latter."

"Would you all stop talking about Gabriel and me having sex?" I make my way to the end of the table and take the empty seat next to Leah. "Leah, tell your wicked mother-in-law to chill," I say, sliding my coat and scarf off and hanging them on the back of the chair. Ever since Leah and Nikolai got married, we all like to tease

Glory by calling her the wicked mother-in-law or mommy dearest. It gets on her nerves big time.

"Now that's just straight up uncalled for." Glory sniffs.

Leah and I share a look before bursting out laughing.

"Can we not talk about *mi hermano* having sex," Leyna butts in. "It's making my skin crawl." She mocks shivers.

"Another round, ladies?" Charley sets down a pitcher of margarita mix on the table then makes his way around to me. "Here ya go, sweetheart. I made yours a virgin."

"Thanks, Charley." I smile up at the older man. Charley's is not the kind of bar that serves margaritas or what the guys like to call girly drinks, but he has always made an exception for us.

"If you ladies don't need anything else, I'm going to head to the back to take the stock before I open. When I get finished, I'll fire up the grill for ya."

Just the thought of one of Charley's bacon and Swiss burgers has my mouth-watering.

"We're all set, Charley. Thanks," Bella tells him.

With a nod, Charley makes his way down the hall to the stockroom.

"So, how long are you and Lex in town for?" Grace asks Leyna.

"Lex and I will stay through Christmas then spend New Year's with his family," Leyna answers.

I look at Leyna and grin. "I'm just glad Gabriel and Lex have finally gotten to the point where they can be in the same room and not want to kill each other."

Leyna shakes her head. "I have never met anyone as pig-headed as mi hermano."

"We heard you got your first teaching position." Mila looks at Leyna.

A huge smile takes over my sister-in-law's face. "I did. I'll be teaching third grade. The position doesn't start until after the summer, in September, but I'm excited."

"You know, I'm here if you ever need any time on how to handle the little rugrats," Glory offers. "You lucked out. I'm still dealing with all those hormonal little shitheads at the high school. Teenagers are the worst."

"That's because you're gorgeous." I giggle.

"True." Glory takes a sip of her drink.

Just then, our conversation is brought to a halt when the door to the bar opens, followed by the loud, booming voices of several men.

"Shit," Bella hisses at the same time everyone's mood shifts. I know why. It's because the men that just strolled in are wearing cuts. And along with them is an energy that causes an uneasy feeling in the pit of my stomach. On instinct, I reach out and grab hold of Bella's arm.

My sister cuts her eyes to me, taking my hand in hers. "It's okay, Alba."

Two seconds later, the men notice our little group here at the back of the bar.

"Fuck," Glory mutters when the bikers make their way toward us.

"What do we have here?" one of them says as he grabs a chair and plops his seedy-looking butt down beside Glory.

"What's your name?" he asks her.

Glory looks at the man like he's the dirt beneath her shoe. "Sorry, boys. Private party."

The biker smiles at Glory in a way that makes my skin crawl. "Feisty. I like that. Say, does the carpet match the drapes, Red?"

Before Glory has a chance to answer the gross question, everyone's attention shifts to the guy who has his gaze fixed on me as he comes to stand behind my chair. It's also the exact moment Charley appears from down the hall with his phone to his ear. There is only one guess needed as to who he is talking to. "Bar's closed," Charley says when he steps up to our table.

The man who was harassing Glory eyes Charley. "Funny, cause you don't look closed. Now, how about you get my boys and me some beers, old man."

Charley's eyes shift from the man in front of him to the one at my back, and suddenly a knot forms in my stomach when I feel the man pick up a lock of my hair. Bella is quick to react.

"Don't fucking touch her." She swats the man's hand away from me.

And it's at this moment the energy in the room turns dangerous and all of us women know what we have to do.

3

———

# GABRIEL

I lift my hand, bringing the bottle to my lips, and throw back what's left of my beer. I push my chair from the table and stand, the muscles in my lower back instantly feeling the strain of the six-hour tattoo session earlier. I head for the opposite side of the room toward the bathroom. On the way, my phone pings. So do several others, which causes my movement across the room to halt. I pull my phone from the pocket of my cut, swipe my thumb across the screen, and a message from Alba stares me in the face.

**Cariño: Trouble at Charley's**

Every muscle in my body goes rigid. I look across the room at my brothers, all of whom are staring at their phones as well. "Get the same message?" I ask.

"Bella says there's trouble at Charley's." Logan's fingers tap rapidly against his phone screen.

"Same," I, along with Quinn, say simultaneously.

"A group of unfriendly bikers is causing trouble." Logan shoves the phone into his back pocket and stands at the same time as Lex, who must have gotten a message from my sister.

"Quinn, Reid, Blake. You ride with Logan," Jake barks as he

17

moves toward the door. "Austin and Gray, we're riding with Gabriel." Jake flings open the front door, and a blast of cold air rushes inside. We file outside. I look over to see Lex already peeling away from the clubhouse.

In less than a minute, we're loading in my SUV and Logan's truck. As soon as the engine turns over, I press the gas pedal into the floorboard. The tires spin, kicking up loose gravel on the frozen ground as I speed away from the clubhouse. The cab of the vehicle falls deathly quiet. Like me, my brothers are in their heads, worried about the women. My grip tightens on the steering wheel until my knuckles turn white. Charley's bar is on the other side of town. A lot can happen in the time it will take us to get there. My mind races with the potential danger Alba is facing. Logan's truck veers left, taking a back road that bypasses going through town. His speed increases and I accelerate with him. There are three feet of snow banks on both sides of the street from the heavy snowfall we've had in the past weeks. I keep my pace with Logan and steady control of the steering wheel as my tires hit a slick patch of ice.

Out of the corner of my eye, I notice Jake glancing at the phone in his hand. "Any word?" I ask.

"Nothin'," Jake says, still staring at his phone.

A vibration radiates from my core as waves of rage pulsate through me. If one of those fuckers touches my woman...

Charley's bar comes into view. I scan the parking lot. Aside from the women's vehicles and Lex, who pulled in ahead of us, I spot an old van parked on the far side of the building. Everyone exits their vehicles and Jake motions for us to scope out the property. When we've finished, the nine of us converge at the side of the building. Jake looks at Logan. "You, Reid, Sam, and Quinn make your way inside through the back entrance. I want these bastards covered from all sides." Logan nods, and he and the guys walk around to the backside of the building. Jake looks at Grey.

"You and Blake keep us covered from the outside while Gabriel, Austin, and I go through the front door."

"You got it, Prez." Grey nods.

Jake turns to me. "Ready?"

I roll my shoulders and crack my neck, eager to inflict pain on some sorry motherfucker. "Let's do this," I growl and fall in behind my President as he swings open the front door.

My eyes quickly adjust from the bright light outside to the dimly lit barroom as we stroll inside. After a quick scan of the space, I count five bikers, including one standing at the bar, with his back to us with a clear view of the MC logo on the back of his leather cut. At the back of the room, Charley has his shotgun in hand, ready to shoot. I look past the motherfuckers standing between our women and us, spotting Alba sitting beside Bella. Her concerned-filled eyes fall on mine. Alba rests her hand against her swollen belly and mouths, *I'm okay.* I won't rest easy until she, along with the others, are safe. I let my sight linger a beat longer in her face before shifting my attention to the group of bikers once more.

One of the men makes a slight move.

"I told you sorry sons of bitches not to move." Charley widens his stance and puts the ugly fucker in his crosshairs.

My eyes cut to Logan, Reid, and Quinn, who stroll up behind the bikers with weapons aimed. "Keep those fuckin' hands where we can see them." Logan's booming voice causes our unwanted guests to spin around in surprise.

"My men are just havin' a little fun—no harm done," the lone biker sitting at the bar says. He then turns and faces Jake, Austin, and me. He's a big motherfucker—built like a linebacker. The patch on the chest of his cut reads President.

"You and your men were asked to leave. We're here to make sure you do." Jake folds his arms across his chest. The Royal Vipers

President eyes him for a beat. Picking up his glass from the bar, he downs what's left of his drink.

"Roll out," he barks, then strolls in our direction, stopping for a moment in front of Jake.

I cut my eyes from the President back to his men who move to follow him—all except for one, who hesitates. The ugly biker with long black hair, who has been eyeballin' me since we arrived, turns his head, glancing back at Alba. My hands fist at my sides and I get tunnel vision—my focus solely on the motherfucker, anticipating his next move. His beady eyes sweep over Alba.

I don't like it.

The bastard looks back at me with a smug smirk.

That's all it takes.

In a few strides, I'm across the room, grabbing him by the collar of his cut. I slam his body against the wall and wrap my hand around his thick neck. "Look her way again, and I'll gut you like the pig you are."

"Fuck you," the asshole speaks with a menacing tone.

Darkness washes over me. "Get the women out of here." I struggle to keep control.

"Oh. Shit," Quinn murmurs and gathers the women.

I feel Alba's eyes on me as she walks past, but I don't glance in her direction. I won't have her see the evil I keep buried inside. I wait for Quinn and Reid to escort the women out the back of the bar before allowing myself to take things further.

"Get control of your man." I hear the president's order.

"Too late," Jake tells him.

The fucker in my grasp doesn't attempt to break free. His icy eyes lock on mine. "You're a dead man," I tell him.

"Not if I kill you first," he sneers, then brings his hand up. I feel the blade I didn't notice beforehand sink into the flesh of my forearm, but his attempt to loosen my hold on him doesn't have the outcome he is looking for.

I feel like I'm outside of my body.

My hand squeezes his throat, putting more pressure against his windpipe. Then, I beat him.

My fist pummels him repeatedly until I feel his facial bones crunch. His face is a broken, bloody mess and my hands are coated in his blood. The piece of shit looks at me through blood-stained eyes. I see his fear.

I smell it as piss puddles at his feet.

And I feed off it.

He's hurt, but I keep going. I need to make sure the bastard can't move by the time I'm done with him. I grip the handle of the knife he drove into my forearm and remove it. Numb with rage and hate, I feel no pain from the open wound left behind.

*"Decirle al diablo que dije hola."* I feel the slight resistance against the tip of the knife as I stab him with his own weapon and revel in the bastard's strangled wails of pain.

"Gabriel!" Jake's sharp voice breaks through, and I jerk my head in his direction. "Enough," he orders. I hesitate before releasing my hold, then take a step back. His body slides down the wall and slumps to the floor. I watch the rise and fall of his chest and stare at the knife stuck in his gut. I could have killed the bastard, but he isn't dead. *Pity.* I should have. "Pick your trash off the floor and get the fuck out of my town," Jake growls.

The Royal Vipers don't make a move until their president nods. Two men lift the beaten piece of shit off the barroom floor and carry his unconscious body out the front door.

"This isn't over." The President squares off in a stare-down with Jake.

"I catch you or your men in Polson again, you'll be digging your graves," Jake warns him, not blinking until the asshole President turns and walks out of the bar. Jake calls out, "Logan, you and a few others tail them. Make sure they leave town for good." Jake strides across the room, stalling in front of me. "You good?"

"I will be."

Understanding, Jake nods. His eyes fall to my arm. "Take care of that, then let's get the women back to the clubhouse."

While Jake briefly talks with Charley, I walk to the restroom and wash my hands. No emotions run through me as the blood of another man rinses down the drain, mixing with my own from the stab wound on my arm. I grab a wad of paper towels from the dispenser and press it against the wound. Luckily, it isn't too deep, but it will need snitches. I rip the hem of my shirt off and tie it around my forearm to keep the paper towels in place over the wound. I stare at my reflection in the mirror for a beat until I no longer see the darkness in my eyes then open the door. Striding out, I go in search of my woman. I notice Sam standing guard at the back entrance. He spots my arm and the blood soaking through the paper towels.

"You okay?"

"I'm good."

Sam jerks his chin toward the end of the hallway. "Quinn and Reid have them in the breakroom."

I roll my sleeve down to hide my wound and walk away, with only one thing on my mind—Alba.

I stand in the doorway of the breakroom, and my eyes fall on Alba sitting with Bella. Feeling my presence, she turns. Relief washes over her face, and she stands. "Gabriel," she sighs. My arms open to her, and she walks into them, pressing her face into my chest. I look at Quinn and Reid. "Prez says to load the women up and get them to the clubhouse."

"You heard the man." Quinn presses off the wall.

I turn my attention away from Alba to seek out Leyna, who I find on the other side of the breakroom in Lex's arms. Lex and I eye each other and I give him a curt nod.

. . .

Almost an hour later, everyone is settled in at the clubhouse. As Doc stitches me up, Alba sits at my side. "I'm sorry."

"Not your fault."

She sighs. "I know. But..."

"Done." Doc puts the last stitch in and eyes Alba, who's rubbing her back. "You doin' alright, sweetheart?"

"Yeah." Alba laughs softly. "I'm at the point in this pregnancy my body aches all the time, is all."

Quinn pops his head through the crack of the half-opened door. "Church." Then he disappears.

Doc moves across the room, putting away his medic supplies. I stand and pull Alba to stand as well. "I won't be long." I kiss her forehead.

My brothers and I are sitting around the table listening to Jake retell us what went down at the bar, but from Charley's perspective. No one, including Charley, has heard of the Royal Vipers until today. As he talks, I find it hard to concentrate on anything but what Alba told me on the drive to the compound and the fact the bastard I left bloodied placed his filthy hands on her. *I regret not killin' the motherfucker.*

"Gabriel," Jake calls my name, and I look across the table at him. "You with us, brother?"

"Sorry."

Jake's attention lingers on me for a second longer before he looks around the room. "Until we find out more about the Royal Vipers, I want all of you to be vigilant. Every family member must be accompanied by a brother until further notice in case of retaliation." Jake looks directly at Reid. "See what you can dig up on this MC—where they're located, names..." Jake falls silent and leans back in his chair, then looks at his watch. "It's getting late."

He slams the gavel against the surface of the table. "Go home with your families. We'll meet back here tomorrow."

A short time later, Alba and I are pulling into the driveway of our home. Gabe's face squished against the living room window's glass helps wash the remaining day's stress away. Alba giggles at our son. "He's excited. I called to check on them earlier and promised him that we would watch The Grinch tonight if he took a bath and cleaned his room. After the day we've both had, I'd say a family movie night is just what we need."

Getting out, I walk around to the passenger side and help Alba out of the vehicle. Once inside, we are attacked by the munchkin. "Papi!" Gabe barrels into my legs, and I hoist him into my arms.

"Hey, *hijo*. Were you good today?"

"Yep." He nods, and I pull open my coat. Gabe reaches into the inside pocket and pulls out a bag of sour candies.

"Not until after dinner." Alba stops him before Gabe opens the candy bag.

I set Gabe down, and he takes off toward the living room. Emma appears and hands Val over to Alba. "Thanks for staying longer," Alba expresses her gratitude.

"It was no problem." Emma grabs her coat and pulls it on. "See you later, Val." She tickles our daughter's side, making her giggle and squirm.

"Gabe, come tell Emma goodbye," Alba calls out.

Bare feet slap against the wood floor as Gabe runs back in our direction. He pops his head around the doorframe. "Bye, Emma." In a flash, he's gone.

Emma laughs. "If I only had half his energy..."

"You and me both." Alba laughs with her.

I dig out my wallet and pull out some cash, handing it to Emma.

"That's too much, Mr. Martinez." She tries giving some back.

"Take it. You worked extra hours today. Consider the rest a Christmas bonus," I tell her, knowing she could use the extra cash.

"Thanks—really." Emma shoves the cash into her bag and tosses it over her shoulder.

Once Emma is gone, I set the alarms, locking the house up for the night. "Why don't you go take a relaxing shower. I'll whip up some grub and get the movie ready."

Alba raises her brow. "You cook?" She passes Val to me.

"What should I order?" I fight to hide my grin.

"Pizza," Alba says, then closes the small distance between us and tugs on my beard, pulling my face down so my lips can meet hers in a kiss.

4
———

# ALBA

Blinking my eyes open, I look over at the clock on the bedside table. It's only four o'clock in the morning but waking up before the sun has become a regular occurrence these past couple of months. I was restless like this when I was pregnant with Gabe and Val. Especially toward the end. Not only do I have to use the restroom a dozen times a night, but it's nearly impossible to find a comfortable position to lay in that doesn't give me back pain. I wouldn't change any of it for the world, though. Turning my head, I look at the man sleeping beside me. We have been married for a few years now, but Gabriel still takes my breath away. I love moments like this when he's asleep. His usually hardened features look almost soft. It's the kind of softness I only witness when he's sleeping or when he looks at our children or me. It's a look that belongs to only us. It's unique in a way that makes me keep moments like this locked away inside my heart for safekeeping. Reaching up, I lightly run the tips of my fingers across his cheek and through his beard.

Suddenly my thoughts drift back to the day before and the incident at Charley's. Gabriel didn't say much about what went down, but I could feel the tension rolling off him in waves all night. Not wanting to wake him, I slide out of bed and pad over to the bathroom. Once the door quietly clicks shut, I turn the light on then head straight for the shower. After turning the water on, I let it heat while I strip out of my t-shirt and panties. When the bathroom fills with steam, I step into the stall and close my eyes as the hot water beats down on my back. A moment later, the shower door opens.

"Cariño," Gabriel's husky voice rumbles. Already naked, he steps in behind me.

"Did I wake you?" I ask.

Gabriel grabs the bottle of shampoo, and I face him as he squeezes some into the palms of his hands then begins to lather my hair.

"I'm sorry if I did. I know you were exhausted when we got home last night." I close my eyes and let out a groan at the feel of his fingers massaging my scalp. "That feels good."

"I heard the shower runnin'. I have an early appointment this morning for a guy who's driving in from Denver. His piece will probably take all day to finish."

After rinsing the shampoo and conditioner from my hair, Gabriel motions for me to sit on the tiled bench. Once I do, he swipes the shaving gel and razor from the shelf. Going down to one knee, he takes one of my legs and props my foot on his thigh. Leaning back against the shower wall, I relax while he carefully shaves my legs. "You spoil me." I smile.

Gabriel's hand pauses, and he lifts his head, pinning his dark eyes on me. "You deserve to be spoiled, Mi Amor." A beat later, he turns his attention back to the task at hand. "What are your plans today?" he asks.

"I have a client who needs me to put together a cover for her, and then I'm meeting Sofia in town for some last-minute shopping with the kids. Gabe said he wanted to get something for Papi."

Gabriel doesn't stop what he's doing, but I don't miss the grin on his face.

"Sam mentioned last night you and Sofia would be going out today. He agreed to tag along," Gabriel supplies.

"Is everything okay?" I ask.

"Prez is being extra cautious after what happened yesterday. I'm sure everything will be fine, but for peace of mind, Sam will hang with you and Sofia today."

"Okay, by me." I smile. "The kids will be happy to spend some time with Uncle Sam."

Later that morning, when Gabriel walks in through the front door, I'm standing at the stove with Val clung to my hip while I make pancakes. The news said we have a big winter storm coming in on Christmas Eve, so Gabriel has been chopping firewood, making sure we will be prepared in case the power goes out. Shrugging his coat off, he hangs it on the hook by the door then makes his way into the kitchen. As soon as he steps next to me, Val reaches her arms out to him. Without hesitation, Gabriel takes his daughter into his arms. "Come here, Princesa." Val lays her head on Gabriel's shoulder. She is definitely a daddy's girl. If the two of us are in a room together, she will always choose Papi over Mommy.

"Do you want to eat before you go?"

Gabriel nods then sits down at the kitchen table where Gabe is currently devouring his fourth pancake. My little guy can pack away some food. He's already taller than most boys his age, and I have a feeling I'll need a second job by the time he's a teenager just to pay for our grocery bill.

Gabriel ruffles his son's hair. "You good today, *hijo*?"

"Yes, sir," Gabe tells his Papi just before stuffing another bite of food into his mouth.

"Mommy is taking you and your sister out today. I want you to look out for them. Can you do that for me?"

Gabe sits up straighter in his chair and regards his father. "Yes, sir. I'll take good care of mommy and Val. I promise."

"Good," Gabriel grunts. "I knew I could count on you, big man."

One thing I can say about Gabe is he is so much like Gabriel. He also takes whatever task his father gives him seriously. And by the way Gabriel is looking at his son he's proud of the fact.

An hour later, there is a knock at the door, followed by Sam and Sofia walking in. Val, still in Gabriel's arms, lets out an ear-piercing squeal when she sees Sam. Like I said, my kids love their Uncle Sam.

"Brother." Sam gives Gabriel a chin lift. "Hey there, munchkin." He gives Val a broad smile as he takes her from Gabriel. He then walks over to where I'm sitting at the table and kisses my cheek. "Little momma."

"Hi, Sam." I look around him to Sofia and beam. "Hi. You guys want breakfast?"

"Naw, we already ate," Sam answers.

Standing from the table, Gabriel takes his cut from the back of the chair and shrugs it on. "I'm headin' out, baby." He strides around the table, leans over, and kisses me. "I'll call and check on you in a bit."

"Okay," I breathe.

After kissing me one last time, Gabriel turns toward Sam. "A word." He jerks his chin toward the door. Nodding, Sam passes Val off to Sofia.

"So, I guess you heard Sam will be tagging along today," Sofia says after the guys step outside.

Not wanting to say anything in front of Gabe, I look at him. "Why don't you go get cleaned up before we go Christmas shopping for Papi."

Nodding his head vigorously, Gabe darts out of his chair and up the stairs. Once he is out of earshot, I turn back to Sofia. "Yeah. I'm not surprised, though. Not after what happened yesterday."

"Me either. To tell you the truth, Sam being there will make me feel better. Yesterday was a little scary."

"I agree. And having Sam with us will make me feel better, too."

"Did Gabriel tell you anything about why they think the other MC is in town?"

I shake my head. "No. But you know they're not going to say much."

Sofia sighs. "I know. Sam was tight-lipped, too."

"I trust the guys. They won't let anything happen. I'm sure it's all nothing. Those bikers were probably just passing through town." Reaching across the table, I give Sofia's arm a light squeeze.


A couple of hours later, we're standing in a small department store. "Have you decided what you want to get?" I look down at Gabe. My little boy has been studying the glass display case for more than twenty minutes. We decided to drive to a small town just outside of Polson to shop. Gabe was very specific about what he wanted to get his Papi for Christmas. He currently has his sights set on an old-fashioned pocket watch with a chain attached.

"I want that one." He taps his little finger on the glass case, showing to the salesman which one he wants.

"You got it, young man." The older gentleman uses a key to unlock the case and takes out the watch Gabe picked. "Would you like it engraved?" he asks.

"Really? You do that here, or does it have to be sent off? It's a Christmas gift, and we'd hate for it to not be ready in time."

"Yes, ma'am. I'll do it myself and can have it ready in about an hour."

Crouching down to eye level with Gabe, I ask, "Do you want to put a special message to Papi on the watch?"

Gabe thinks for a moment, then nods. "Yes."

Ten minutes later, we walk out of the shop. "Well, we have an hour to kill. How about some lunch?" Sam suggests.

"You don't have to ask me twice." I rub my belly.

"You're in luck, little momma." Sam grins. "There's a Mexican place across the street."

I follow his line of sight. "And it's Tuesday."

"It will be just like old times." He chuckles.

It's late afternoon by the time we pick up Gabriel's Christmas present and finish the rest of our shopping.

"I'm going to stop off at the gas station and fill up." Sam eyes me through the rearview mirror of his truck.

Sofia twists in her seat, looking back at me and then the kids, who are both fast asleep. "No wonder it's so quiet."

I laugh. "Yeah, they should sleep the whole way home."

"Fuck," Sam hisses, drawing Sofia's and my attention.

"What is it?" I ask, but my question is answered when, suddenly, three men on motorcycles pull up alongside Sam's truck. I look out my window to see a man wearing a cut with the same insignia as the bikers from Charley's.

"Sam." My voice comes out shaky.

One of the motorcycles cuts over in front of us, making Sam swerve to the side of the road. I look over at Val, who thankfully is still asleep, but when my eyes travel away from my daughter to Gabe, I see he is wide awake, his little hands balled into fists. He stares out his window at the men chasing us and then looks back at me. "Mommy, what's going on?" Reaching across the seat, I take one of his hands in mine. "It's going to be okay, sweetheart."

"Son of a bitch," Sam grinds out. "Hold on," he orders just as he slams his foot down on the accelerator. Then I watch as he places his phone to his ear.

**5**

---

# GABRIEL

Before heading to Kings Ink, I pull into Kings Custom to check in with Jake and find out if the new set of tires I ordered has arrived. The brutal winter winds cut through me like a knife the moment I step out of the truck. Fuck. I stomp my feet through the slush and snow and enter the storefront, finding Bella inside behind the counter, tapping away at the computer. She looks up from her work and smiles. "Hey, big guy."

"Logan in?" I bring my cold hands to my mouth and blow hot breath on them to warm my skin.

"He's in the shop fixing one of the bike lifts," she says. Giving her a nod, I turn on my heels and head to his location. I find him bent over the generator with wrenches in hand. Hearing my boots against the concrete floor, Logan looks up. "Hey, brother. What brings you by this morning?" he asks, looking back at his task.

"Just stoppin' to see about that set of snow tires. I'd like to get them on the truck before the snowstorm hits."

Logan tosses the socket in his hand and picks up another tool lying beside him. "They came in yesterday. If you leave your ride here, I can have the tires swapped out before noon," he says.

"That works for me." I dig my keys out of my front pocket. "Here," I say. Logan looks up as I toss him the keys and catches them. I glance at the clock hanging on the wall and notice I should get to work before my appointment arrives. Before I take my leave, I ask, "Any word on the Royal Vipers yet?"

"Reid is still working on it." Logan searches around for a bottle of hydraulic fluid. "We're all on alert, brother."

"I know." Still, it isn't enough to settle my nerves and the knot in my stomach that hasn't gone away since the club sent those dickheads down the road.

"Who's with Alba and the kids today?" He eyes me.

"Sam."

"Good." Logan pauses a beat, then adds, "We all feel the same, brother. Prez has Austin and Blake cruisin' town today. If they see something, we will know. And Charley closed the bar for a few days, but he's keepin' his eyes open also. As soon as I know something, we all know something."

Several hours later, I'm wrapping up the final touches on my client's piece. Turning, I grab a bottle off the table and rinse off his skin. "Alright, man. You know the routine." I push my chair away, and he gets up from the table. He steps in front of the mirror to get a look at the work I've put in for the past seven hours.

"Fuck, man." He steps closer to look at the fine lines. "The details on the dragon are sick." He turns and walks back, and I cover his fresh ink with a transparent bandage.

I forgo the entire aftercare speech since a large portion of his body is covered in ink—many of which I have done myself over the past couple of years. I throw all the used equipment away, then remove and toss my gloves into the nearby trash can.

"Thanks, man. Hope you and the family have a good

Christmas." He extends his hand, and I shake it, then he shrugs his coat on.

"You too," I say, knowing he's heading to his wife and kids back in Denver.

Once he's exited the building, I finish cleaning my station. Like always, I do a final walkthrough, turning off the lights before heading out. I step out into the bitter cold and lock the door, then look up at the snow clouds beginning to blanket the sky. I shove my hands into my coat pockets and make my way across the street toward the bike shop where I left my SUV earlier in the day. My vehicle is sitting in the parking lot with the new set of tires on it. Logan notices me walking up as he steps out the front door with Bella.

"Hey, brother. I was just about to swing by and drop off your keys." He locks the shop up, then fishes my keys from his jacket pocket. "I changed the oil for ya, too." He tosses the key my way.

"Appreciate it."

My phone rings, and I retrieve it from the back pocket of my jeans. Seeing Sam's number on the screen causes my entire body to stiffen. "Brother," I answer the phone. The strain in my voice catches Logan and Bella's attention.

"Those sons of bitches are back. I need backup." Sam's tone is urgent. "Shit!" Sam curses. In the background, I can hear my son's terror-filled cries asking his momma what's happening, and my stomach bottoms out.

"Where are you?" I'm moving toward my vehicle, and Logan is right behind me.

"We're nearing the highway bridge out here by the lake." Sam's voice becomes distant, but I hear him say, "Get down!" followed by the unmistakable sound of bullets piercing metal.

I feel all the blood drain from my face as I look at Logan. "My family is in trouble."

Bella grasps at her chest, and her eyes pool with unshed tears.

"My sister and the kids," she chokes on her words. Logan quickly faces his woman,

"Go. I want all the families at the clubhouse." He quickly kisses Bella, who then eyes me for a fraction of a second before rushing to her car and peeling out of the parking lot. Logan jumps into the passenger's seat of my truck as I get behind the wheel. Logan is on the phone before the engine starts, and I'm peeling away from the bike shop toward the location Sam gave. My fingers grip the steering wheel, damn close to ripping the fucker off as I listen to Logan relay to Jake our situation. "Where are they?" Logan faces me.

"Near the highway bridge by the lake," I say, and Logan repeats their location. "More brothers are on the way," Logan says, tossing his phone into the center console. He then reaches beneath his jacket and cut, pulling out his weapon. "There isn't anywhere for them to go between here and the clubhouse. The others will run into them unless we get there first."

Once I'm out of city limits and on an open road, I gun it. The sound of tires vibrating against the road becomes the only sound making it easier for me to get lost in my head. Thoughts of losing my family start flooding my mind, and I roar with rage. "Fuck!"

Within seconds of my outburst, the tail end of the vehicle Alba is in comes into view as I crest a small hill. Sam's truck swerves, clipping one of the bikers, sending him crashing against the railing of the bridge. The two remaining keep chasing. Giving my truck more gas, I close the gap between us and the bikers. Logan rolls down his window, leans out, takes aim, and fires his gun. A second biker goes down. I swerve to avoid hitting the Harley as it skids across the highway. I watch one of the Royal Vipers aim his gun at the vehicle holding my family. Though Sam has managed to put some distance between them, the biker can shoot out a tire, causing Sam's truck to swerve into a snowbank piled against a cluster of trees.

I won't stop.

"This ends today," I growl and press the gas pedal into the floor, forcing my truck to give me all it has to get up close to the last two remaining Vipers before he makes it to my family. As I get up beside him on the opposite side of the road, I run my truck into him. Metal impacts metal. I hold onto the steering wheel as my tires lose traction and we begin spinning. My first thought when we finally stop is getting to Alba and my kids. I look over at Logan.

"Go." He proceeds to crawl out of the passenger window because his door is jammed. Flinging open the driver's door, I jump from the truck and run several yards down the road where Sam's truck sits. I throw open the back door, finding Sophia, Alba, and my kids, hunkered down on the floor, with Sam, gun in hand, ready to defend them.

"Thank fuck." Relief washes over me as my family looks at me.

"Papi!" Gabe's eyes are round with fear as he clutches onto his momma. Alba locks eyes with me, keeping a tight hold on our children.

"Gabriel." Her voice trembles.

"You hurt?"

Alba shakes her head. "No. We're all okay. Scared but unharmed."

The sound of approaching vehicles draws my attention. I turn my head and look back at the road to see some of our brothers pulling up to the scene. I want desperately to scoop my wife and kids into my arms, but I need to make sure the Royal Vipers will no longer pose a threat. I look at Sam. "I owe you."

"No. You don't." His words are firm. "We take care of our own. Your family is my family. I will bleed for them."

I regard him and his statement for a beat, then give him a nod. "Take them to the clubhouse."

"You got it."

Jake rolls up in the van with Quinn and Austin in tow. Grey

pulls in behind him in his truck. "Grey," I wave him over. "I need you and Sam to take my family back to the clubhouse."

"Sure thing," Grey says.

I grab Gabe from Alba after helping her out of the truck. Gabe tries looking past my shoulder at the wreckage behind us, but I stop him. "Look forward, *hijo*," I order, and he doesn't hesitate in listening. I lead them to Grey's ride and wait for him and Sam to secure the car seats into the truck's back seat. I place the kids inside, buckle them in, face my woman once more, and touch her cheek. "I need to take care of something. You and the kids stay with Sam."

"Gabriel..." Alba leans into my touch. "Please come home alive."

"I will."

"Promise?" Alba stares up at me.

"Promise." Kissing her, I help her onto the seat, buckle her in and close the door.

Once Grey and Sam pull away from the scene, I turn and walk in the direction of the others standing off the side of the road. I come to a stop beside Jake and stare down at one of the assholes I hit. It's the same motherfucker I beat the shit out of at Charley's. "He's still breathing."

"And he'll stay that way until we get done with him," Jake states.

I look around, not seeing the other fuckers we took out. "And the others?"

"One is dead, and the other is busted up but alive." Jake looks around and lets out a heavy sigh. "Toss the two still breathing in the van and take them to the shed. I don't want the trash anywhere near our families."

Night has fallen by the time we've cleaned the scene and gotten the two Royal Vipers to the old shed on the backside of the compound. So have the temperatures outside. Jake decides to deal with them first thing in the morning and calls Doc down from the clubhouse.

Doc strolls in, carrying two syringes.

"You're all dead men," the less injured Viper sneers, his teeth chattering from the cold.

Doc injects them with a sedative to keep them quiet through the night.

I lock eyes with the fucker. His face is still bruised and swollen from the beating I gave him the other day. "You can't threaten death on someone who walks with the devil himself. Come tomorrow, you'll wish I'd killed you two days ago."

6

## ALBA

I wake up and reach out to Gabriel's side of the bed only to find it cold. After what happened yesterday, the club made the decision to bring everyone to the clubhouse. To say the tension surrounding the guys was thick would be an understatement. It was a struggle to keep my own feelings in check when we got back yesterday, but I managed to keep it together for the kids. Val was oblivious to what went down, but Gabe knew something was wrong. After we got the kids down last night, Gabriel brought me into our room here at the clubhouse, and that was when I finally let everything I was holding in out. I don't know how long I spent crying in his arms. I was terrified for my children, and what happened also brought up some bad memories. The club has been no stranger to the kinds of situations we experienced yesterday, but it was like opening old wounds. And not just for me, but Gabriel was feeling the effects as well. Only this time, our children were also the ones in danger.

Sitting up in bed, I ignore the soreness in my back and scoot to the edge until my feet touch the floor. The moon still shines brightly through the window, and the clock on the bedside table says it's a few minutes past three o'clock in the morning. Standing, I go in search of my husband, though I have a pretty good idea where he is. I make the short trek to the bedroom across the hall, and sure enough, I find Gabriel sitting in a chair beside the bed where Gabe and Val are sleeping. I take a moment to study him. Gabriel's face is like stone, but his dark eyes have always told me all I need to know. He's struggling to not lose it.

"Come here, Cariño," Gabriel rumbles without taking his eyes off the kids.

I amble toward him and take his hand when he holds it out, then he pulls me down to his lap. Closing my eyes, I rest my head against his chest. My body relaxes the moment he closes his arms around me.

"Have you slept at all?" I ask, already knowing the answer.

"No."

We're both quiet for a beat.

"How's my baby doin'?" Gabriel rubs his large hand over my belly.

"Good." I smile against his chest. Lifting my head, I look at his pained face. "We're okay, Gabriel. The kids are okay." I palm his cheek.

Gabriel stares into my eyes. He doesn't speak a word, but his gaze is telling me a million different things.

"Come back to bed. You need to get some rest." When Gabriel still doesn't say anything, I try again. "Please. I sleep better when you're next to me."

That gets him. Gabriel's face goes soft. Slipping one arm beneath my legs and the other around my back, he cradles me against his chest and stands. Carefully and with ease, Gabriel carries me back into our bedroom and gently lays me down on the bed. I watch as he strips out of his cut, t-shirt, and jeans before crawling into bed behind me, where he wraps his arm around my swollen belly, making me feel safe and content.

"Sleep, Cariño," are the last words I hear before drifting off.

***

Hours later, I walk into the kitchen with Val and Gabe to find Lisa, Ember, and Raine busy cooking breakfast.

"Good morning, Alba."

At the sound of Ember's greeting, Lisa turns away from the stove and smiles. "Hey, guys. You're just in time." She wipes her hands on a towel and beams down at Gabe, who is holding his sister's hand. "Hey, handsome. Are you hungry?"

Gabe smiles up at Lisa and nods.

"Come on and sit down. I'll fix you all a plate," she tells us.

"You don't have to do that, Lisa. I can get it," I protest.

"Nonsense. You know I live for this sort of thing. Now, come on and sit."

I know better than to argue with Lisa. She's right; she does live to take care of everyone. When she has the kids served and a plate in front of me, Bella, Grace, and Mila walk into the kitchen together with Bree, Jake, Ava, and Noah, Remi, and Ellie in tow.

"Good morning," my sister says, then ushers the kids to sit at the table beside Gabe and Val.

"Morning," I mumble around a bite of food.

Ten minutes later, Emerson and her daughter, along with Sofia, join us. We all sit and eat our breakfast together in comfortable silence until all the guys come walking into the kitchen. Lisa, Ember, and Raine jump up and begin serving them some food. There is obvious tension rolling off the men, but luckily Lisa comes to the rescue.

"You know, I have a whole bunch of Christmas decorations up in my attic. How about I get Bennett to bring it all to the clubhouse, and we spend the day decorating."

"Yay!" is the chorus of responses we get from all the kids.

"And I bet we can also get him to wrangle us up a tree, too," she adds.

"Can we hang lights too?" Ellie, Jake and Grace's daughter, ask.

"Of course." Lisa ruffles her hair. "We've got to have lights. I'll even go to the store and get stuff to make cookies and hot chocolate."

Me, Bella, Mila, Grace, and Emerson give Lisa an appreciative look. This is just what the kids need to keep their minds preoccupied.

Bennett jumps up from the table. "I guess I better get busy then."

"Raine and I are going to make a run to the craft store," Ember announces. "We promised the kids we'd help them make some homemade Christmas stockings."

"That sounds like fun. Thank you, guys." I smile at Raine and Ember.

"We're going to get ready. If any of you need anything, just make a list, and we'll pick it up while we're out," Ember adds. "You too, Lisa. Just make a list, and we'll take care of it."

Lisa gives Ember and Raine a hug. "You two are lifesavers. Thank you."

Later that afternoon, I'm sitting with Bella in the main room of the clubhouse when Glory walks through the door. "Let's get the Christmas party started." She holds up two bottles of wine. "Oh, and I come bearing gifts."

Walking in behind Glory are Victor and Sasha, carrying a huge tree.

Bella and I stand from the sofa. "Where did you find a tree this close to Christmas?" I ask.

"Demetri heard the kids wanted a tree, and Bennett was having a hard time finding one. So, he sent Victor and Sasha out to find one. Translation, they went into the woods and cut one down."

It's true. Bennett returned to the clubhouse a couple of hours ago, and every tree market he'd gone to hadn't had anything, and the kids were disappointed. Though the way Bella's face lit up when Bennett hauled in several boxes, all filled with decorations she'd bought over the past few years, which Logan claimed mysteriously disappeared, was priceless.

"You guys are the best," I praise.

Just then, all the children come running into the room. Ember and Raine have been doing an excellent job lifting their spirits by working on crafts in the playroom.

"We have a Christmas tree!" Gabe shouts, and all the other kids follow suit, jumping up and down and clapping as they surround Victor and Sasha.

"Is that for us?" my nephew, Jake, asks.

"Yay!" Ellie claps her hands and squeals.

"Can we put the lights on now?" Remi adds.

I notice Glory standing off to the side with a big smile at the kids' excitement, taking a video with her phone. She then taps the screen, no doubt sending the footage to Demetri so he can see Jake and Bree's reaction. Demetri adores his grandchildren.

"Looks like I made it just in time."

I turn toward the voice that just spoke to see Leyna walking into the clubhouse.

"You did." I walk up to her and give her a hug. "Where's Lex?"

"He just dropped me off and is meeting up with the guys."

The two of us share a look then turn our attention back to Victor and Sasha setting up the tree.

"Who's ready to decorate the tree?" Bennett booms, walking into the room carrying several boxes of decorations.

"Me!" all the kids shout. Their excitement is contagious, and I can't help but laugh.

As the kids laugh, play, and begin decorating the tree, I start taking pictures to share with Gabriel. He's been texting me every thirty minutes checking on us, so I figure giving him actual proof will help keep his mind at ease.

"Hey." Emerson sits down on the sofa beside me, nudging me with her shoulder. "How are you holding up? You feeling okay?"

After the incident yesterday, Gabriel insisted Emerson check me out. He was worried about the baby and me, even though I felt pretty good once everything settled down. It wasn't until Emerson brought her equipment to the clubhouse and let Gabriel hear the baby's heartbeat that he calmed down. "I'm doing okay. I just had about a dozen of Lisa's chocolate chip cookies, so the baby is now doing summersaults." I rub my belly and laugh. "I promise if I start feeling off, I'll let you know. But other than having to pee every ten minutes and a sore back, I'm good," I assure her.

Val giggling draws my attention away from Emerson, and the sight in front of me melts my heart. Picking up my phone, I hold it up, capturing the moment Gabe lifts Val up so she can hang a shiny silver ornament on the Christmas tree. When her brother sets her back on her feet, Val runs over to me as fast as her little legs will carry her. "Momma see?" she asks as she climbs onto my lap.

"I see, baby." I nuzzle my face into the crook of her neck, making her squeal.

"Are you having fun?" I ask.

Val nods before climbing down and running back over to her big brother, where he proceeds to help her hang another decoration.

"Hey." Glory plops down on the other end of the sofa. "What are you two talking about?" She looks between Emerson and me.

"I was asking Emerson for advice on the best medication to get rid of my hemorrhoids," I answer with a straight face.

"Jesus Christ, Alba. Forget I asked." Glory pushes off the sofa and walks away while mumbling how disgusting pregnancy is. I look over at Emerson and the two of us burst out laughing.

"She is too easy to mess with." I shrug.

"You're crazy, Alba." Emerson bumps my shoulder again. "Don't ever change."

## 7

## GABRIEL

We've been out here freezing our balls off for hours. I leave the warmth of the gas-generated heater and join my brothers.

I hover above the last biker standing, ready to inflict pain. He glances at his buddy lying on the floor beside him with a bullet in his head. "You willin' to talk before we begin?"

"Fuck you." The asshole spits on my shoe.

I grab a handful of greasy hair and haul him to his feet, slam my fist into his gut, then press his back against the wood panels behind him. My hand wraps around his neck, keeping him in place while my brothers spread his legs and arms, locking them in place. I step away, stroll across the barn, and lift a large pipe wrench from a pile of rusty tools. I sling it over my shoulder and walk back toward our guest.

Jake pulls up a chair and takes a seat in front of the biker. "Where is your club?"

"Suck my dick," the son of a bitch growls through clenched teeth.

I swing the wrench down. You can hear the bones in his leg snap when the metal cracks across his shin. He wails in pain.

"You could make this a lot less painful if you just tell us what we want to know." Jake leans back and folds his arms across his chest. "Your buddy there lasted longer than I expected." Jake jerks his head at the man lying on the floor, and the guy cuts his eyes at his dead brother. "If you're willin' to suffer, my man here is more than happy to accommodate you."

"Give it your best shot." The guy smirks, and I bring the wrench down a second time, crushing the kneecap of his other leg. Bored with the weapon in my hand, I toss it to the side. I step away and retrieve a nail gun. I don't wait for Jake to question him again. Instead, I step up to the biker's left hand and drive three nails into the palm of his hand, then casually stroll to the right and do the same to his other palm.

"Fuck!" he bellows in agony.

A rush of cold air swirls around my feet as the barn doors open. Reid steps inside. "I have a location," he says. "They're holed up in an abandoned cabin at the foothill of the mountain range north of Flathead."

"You sure?" Logan asks, and Reid looks at him.

"One of our sources spotted them less than an hour ago. He tracked them down to the location I just mentioned." Reid pauses when the fucker in my grasp opens his mouth and begins to laugh.

I turn my attention from Reid to the sorry son of a bitch and press the nail gun to his chest. I pull the trigger and drive a 2 ½ inch nail in his chest. His eyes widen. I lower the nail gun to the floor, and on my way up, pull a knife from my boot. I place the blade against his jugular, pausing long enough to look back at Jake. His sharp nod is the answer I need. I face the cocksucker one more time. *"Decirle al diablo que dije hola."* My blade slices through his flesh. Crimson soaks his cut, and he gurgles, choking on his blood. After a few more gasping breaths, life fades from his eyes.

"You've got style, brother." Quinn claps my back.

Jake stands. "We've been out here most of the damn day. It's getting late. Let's clean the shit up and dispose of the trash. I, for one, would like a hot meal and a drink. We'll head out at first light to finish off the rest of the Vipers."

A few hours later, I have Alba sitting on my lap while we all sit around, enjoying a drink and watching the kids as they finish decorating the massive Christmas tree placed in the center of the room. "Val, stop eating the decorations," Alba laughs as our daughter devours the garland made from popcorn. Val giggles, then runs and climbs into Leyna's lap.

"I'm hungry." Gabe pops another kernel in his mouth.

"That boy is always eating." Alba sighs, then rubs at her belly.

"You okay, Mi Amor?"

"Yeah. The baby is very active tonight." She takes hold of my hand and places it where hers is resting. I feel my lips lift at the corners, feeling the movement of our unborn child.

"Mommy, can I listen?" Gabe comes running up to us, carrying the small at-home fetal doppler Emerson gave us.

Alba smiles at our son. "Sure, sweetheart." Alba takes the monitor, lifts her sweater enough to expose her pregnant belly, and moves it around until the steady rhythm of our baby's heartbeat echoes. Alba turns the volume up a bit, and Gabe lays his head against his momma's belly. The chatter stops, and the room falls silent. The only other noises are little giggles from the younger kids playing with the train set circling the tree's base. The whooshing sounds capture almost everyone's attention, and the entire family listens.

I look across the room to where Val is nestled in my sister's lap, sleeping.

I feel content.

For a moment, all our troubles and worries fade.

## 8

## ALBA

I stare out the bedroom window and watch as the snow begins to fall. It's near midnight, officially Christmas Eve, and though my body is beyond exhausted, I can't seem to shut my brain off long enough to fall asleep. The guys have been gone a lot trying to deal with that other club that's hell-bent on causing trouble, while the rest of us do what we can to keep the children happy. So far, we've succeeded. The kids finished decorating the clubhouse, ate their weight in cookies, and drank hot chocolate until they passed out. The guys did make it home in time last night to see the kids put the finishing touches on the tree. It just shows that it doesn't matter where you spend the holidays, but whom you spend that time with. We might be stuck at the clubhouse, but the memories we made yesterday were just as special as all the rest.

The sound of the bedroom door clicking shut draws my attention away from the snowfall and my wandering thoughts.

"Baby." Gabriel walks into the room. He and the other guys have been holed up in church for a while. "Can't sleep?" he asks.

I shake my head. "My body is tired, but my brain is not." Gabriel kicks his boots off by the closet, then slips out of his cut, sitting on top of the dresser. He then peels off his flannel and shucks his jeans, leaving him in nothing but a pair of black boxer briefs. I let my eyes travel the length of his body, and my center clenches at the sight of his hardening cock that's barely contained by the thin layer of fabric.

"Come here," he orders, his voice gruff.

Following his command, I make my way to where he's standing. Once I am in front of him, Gabriel loosens the knot on my silk robe, causing it to fall open, exposing my bare breasts. One of his large hands goes straight for my right breast while the other hand slips inside the front of my panties. Gabriel growls in appreciation when he discovers I'm already wet. I gasp when he runs his middle finger through my slit before pressing down on my swollen clit. "Oh, god."

Gabriel leans forward and nips at my bottom lip. "I love how your pussy is always ready for me."

"Always," I hum while he pumps his finger in and out of me. I feel my arousal running down the inside of my thigh. Too soon, Gabriel pulls away, and I buck my hips in protest. I don't lose his connection for long because he is down on his knees in front of me a moment later, peeling my underwear down my legs. Once I'm bared for him, Gabriel presses his face against me. I nearly come undone when he swipes his tongue along the seam of my pussy. "Gabriel." I grab a fist full of his hair.

Gabriel licks and nips at me until I feel my legs about to give out. Taking me with him, Gabriel stands and sits in the chair behind him. "Ride me."

Bracing my palms on his shoulder, I straddle Gabriel's thighs before slowly sinking onto his cock. With my feet firm against the floor and with Gabriel's hands gripping my hips, I fall into a steady rhythm.

"Fuck," he hisses the same time a throaty, "Yes," escapes past my lips.

"I'm going to come," I announce.

"Come, Cariño. Come all over my cock."

By the time Gabriel growls his command, white flashes of light burst behind my eyelids, and I scream out his name as my orgasm crashes through me. Seconds later, Gabriel buries his face in the crook of my neck. "Fuck," he grinds out just before he gets lost in his own release. I don't know how long we stay in this position, but out of nowhere, exhaustion hits me like a freight train, making my body go lax.

"Let's get you to bed." Gabriel kisses my temple as he stands with me in his arms. I let out a sigh when the cool sheets make contact with my heated skin.

"Sleep, Cariño."

I stir sometime later with a sharp pain in my lower back. Blinking my eyes open, I go to switch positions only to have the pain intensify. "Gabriel," I call out, but when I look beside me, his spot on the bed is empty. With a sigh, I climb from bed and make my way into the bathroom in search of some pain reliever. After popping a couple of pills, I splash some cold water onto my face. Soon enough, the sharp pain disappears. Knowing I won't fall back asleep right away, I decide to go down to the kitchen for some hot tea. After slipping on a pair of sleep shorts and one of Gabriel's t-shirts, I walk across the hall to check on Val and Gabe. Satisfied they won't stir, I make my way down the darkened hallway to the stairs. When I hit the first step, another dull ache hits my lower back. I momentarily wonder if this is more than just typical pregnancy aches and pains, but then quickly shake that thought away. I'm still a couple of weeks out from my due date, and I felt much the same toward the end of my pregnancies with Gabe and Val. By the time I ascend the stairs, the pain has once again disappeared.

Ten minutes later, I carry a steaming mug of tea out of the kitchen and over to the oversized chair situated between the window and the Christmas tree. Bringing the cup to my lips, I look to my right and peer out the window. The snow has gotten heavier, and there looks to already be at least a foot of it covering the ground.

"Hey," a voice calls out.

I turn my head to see my sister at the base of the stairs.

"What are you doing up?" she asks.

I rub my belly and shrug. "You know how it is."

Bella gives me a warm smile. "Yeah."

"What about you? Why are you up?" I counter.

Bella sits down on the sofa and draws her legs up to her chest. "Logan woke me up before he left. I haven't been able to get back to sleep."

I nod. "What time did they leave? Gabriel was already gone when I woke up."

"About an hour ago," Bella supplies. "Logan said they had everything under control, but I still can't help but worry."

"Same," I sigh. "I hate all this is happening. It feels like just as soon as life calms down somewhat, something like this happens."

"Yeah. This is the life we signed up for when we fell in love with one of these men, though. We have to learn to roll with the punches."

My sister and I sit together in comfortable silence for a beat when I notice my tea has turned cold. Looking at Bella, I hold my cup up. "I'm going to get a refill. You want some?"

"Sure." She smiles. "Some tea sounds perfect. I'll go with you."

A strange feeling washes over me when I stand, followed by warm wetness that trickles down my legs. I stare at the puddle forming on the floor at my feet for several long seconds before what's happening clicks.

"Alba, are you coming?" Bella asks when she rounds the sofa and heads in the direction of the kitchen.

I look up from the wet spot on the floor to my sister. "Um, either I just peed myself, or my water just broke," I tell her, my voice surprisingly calm.

"You're kidding." Bella rushes to my side, and her eyes widen when she sees the puddle on the floor. "Oh, shit."

"What's with all the noise?"

Bella and I turn our attention to Glory, standing over by the stairs with her hand covering her mouth as she yawns.

"Alba's water just broke," my sister tells her.

"So. Get her another one," Glory mumbles.

Bella and I look dumbly at her.

Glory looks between me and Bella and blinks. "What?"

I look at my sister and give her a "is she kidding" look. And Bella gives me a "no, this bitch is not kidding" look in return.

I turn my attention back to a still-confused Glory. "The water Bella is talking about is coming from my vag."

Glory continues to give me a strange look until finally, what I'm saying registers. Then her face scrunches. "You didn't have to say it like that."

Glory walks over to where I'm standing and looks down at the floor. The puddle is even bigger now. "I'm not cleaning that. No way am I touching your vag water."

"Really, Glory?" I huff. I go to say something else, but I'm cut off when my entire belly tightens in pain, causing me to double over.

"Contraction?" Bella goes into full-on mama bear mode.

I suck in a sharp breath. "Oh yeah." I take several deep cleansing breaths, breathing in through my nose and out through my mouth.

Bella turns to Glory. "Will you go wake Emerson up? Tell her Alba's water broke, and she's in labor."

Glory nods and quickly retreats up the stairs. She's only gone a minute before she and Emerson make their way back down.

"How long ago did her water break, and how far apart are the contractions?" Emerson fires off.

"Only one contraction so far, and her water broke not even ten minutes ago," Bella answers for me.

"Are you sure you weren't contracting before?" Emerson looks at me.

I shake my head. "I don't think so. I woke up because my back was hurting more than usual. That was over an hour ago." Just as the words leave my mouth, another contraction wracks my body. This time I can't help but cry out as I wrap my arms around my belly. "Ahh!"

"I'm going to call Gabriel," Bella announces.

"I'm going to get Bennett to drive us to the hospital," Emerson follows.

"I'm going to get the wine," Glory tosses out.

"What's going on? We heard someone screaming." Lisa rushes into the room with Bennett on her heels.

"Alba is in labor." Emerson faces Bennett. "Can you drive us to the hospital?"

Bennett rushes toward the door. "I'll bring the truck around. Wait here."

A blast of cold air seeps into the clubhouse when Bennett exits.

"Are you all sure you're going to make it?" Glory asks. "It's really coming down out there." She points out the window.

We all look toward the window, and sure enough, conditions have worsened. Not only are several feet of snow covering the ground, but the wind has picked up.

Bella must sense my nervousness. "It will be okay, Alba." She rubs my back.

"Were you able to get Gabriel on the phone?" I look at my sister with a hopeful gaze.

"No. It went straight to voicemail. I tried calling Logan too but got the same response."

"This can't be happening," I mutter. "Oh, god," I groan when I feel my stomach tightening again.

"Should her contractions be this close together so soon?" Bella asks Emerson.

"What's...?" Mila joins the party. "Oh, shit. Is Alba in labor?"

"Yes," Emerson, Bella, and Glory answer in unison.

"I don't feel too good," I announce, still clutching my belly, my face breaking out in a sweat.

"Come on. I want you to lie down on the sofa." Emerson helps guide me over to lie down. A minute later, Bennett pushes through the front door, covered in snow.

"Bad news. The truck is stuck in the snow."

"Please tell me you're kidding," I grit through yet another contraction.

"Let's try calling an ambulance." Emerson wastes no time getting on the phone. Once she gets someone on the line to explain the situation, her expression turns grim then she walks away while talking in a hushed tone. By the time she hangs up the phone, I can tell I'm not going to like what's about to come out of her mouth.

"There was a pile-up on the highway. They dispatched an ambulance but said it could take a while."

I look at my sister. "Bella."

"You're fine, Alba. Everything will be fine."

"Alright, everyone." Lisa claps her hands together. "We have to face the possibility that Alba is going to be having this baby here."

"I can't do this...." I go to say only to have Lisa cut me off.

"Yes, you can. And you will." Lisa sits down next to me and takes my hand. "You've proven time and time again how strong you are, sweetheart. Now, this may not be the way you envisioned bringing your baby into this world, but this is the hand you've been dealt. You're going to do this for your baby." Lisa looks me in the eyes. "You with me?"

I take a shuddered breath and nod. "Yes. I'm with you. I can do this."

"Damn right you can," Lisa states with conviction.

# 9

## GABRIEL

The weather took a turn for the worse not long after we set out before daybreak this morning. Now, as we approach the Royal Vipers location, the forecasted snowstorm is bearing down on us. Strong gusts of wind rock the SUV, and heavy snowfall makes visibility shit. Bringing the vehicle to a stop, I wait for the others to pull up alongside me in the only road leading to the old, abandoned logging mill before stepping out into the frigid cold. Every man exits the three SUVs and waits for Jake to speak. I glance at all the men here today, ready for yet another battle. Taking no chances of odds being against us, we rode twelve strong. The only member not with us is Doc. We left him and a few of Demetri's men to watch over the families back at the clubhouse. My thoughts drift back to the other day, and the dangerous situation Alba and our kids experienced. If something would have happened to them, I could never forgive myself.

I can't allow myself to go there.

My family is my world.

I will do anything to keep them safe.

"I can't see shit," Quinn says, peering through a pair of binoculars.

We may not have a clear visual of the positioning of the Vipers men, but we do have the advantage of knowing the layout of the property itself. Before leaving the clubhouse, Reid showed us an old aerial view of the land and the two-story building. Old broken logging equipment, along with a rusted-out logging truck, all scattered about the small yard. The place has been inoperable for years. We still have no further information on the club itself, which makes us believe they are a nomad MC. They basically are wanderers who have no roots. "Listen up," Jake commands our attention. "This storm isn't letting up any time soon. I realize we can't see shit, but that means the Royal Vipers can't either." A strong gust of wind pushes hard against our bodies. "The south end of the building is open and exposed. That's our entry point. We roll in hot. Check your weapons. There is no stopping until every Viper is dead. We are here to exterminate them. You got me?"

After a beat of silence and shared looks around the group, we file back into the vehicles. I quickly pull out my phone and notice Logan sitting in the passenger seat, doing the same. I shoot a text to Alba.

**Me: I love you**

None of us ever know what day may be our last. I don't wait for her reply. There is no time. I shove the phone back into my pocket and put the vehicle in drive. The SUV Jake is driving lurches forward, and that's my cue to gun it. From here on, everything happens fast. We barrel toward the building. "Shit!" Bullets shatter my driver-side window, sending shards of glass across my lap. There's a loud pop when another shot pops a front tire causing the SUV to suddenly pull to the right, slamming into a piece of broken machinery a couple of yards from the building.

Logan, Quinn, Nikolai, and I jump from the wrecked vehicle. With guns drawn, we rush toward the fight.

I take aim at one fucker reloading his gun and fire, then watch Logan and Nikolai put bullets in two more men. Once we've made it to the side of the mill, Logan says, "Gabriel, you and Quinn sweep the east side. Sam and I will clear the west end." I nod, then we separate. Keeping our backs against the building, Quinn and I make our way to the property's east side facing the mountain range. I flex the hand wrapped around my weapon, trying to keep my fingers from going numb as the bitter cold continues to penetrate my skin, then blink away the snowflakes sticking to my eyelashes.

A shot rings out.

"Motherfucker!" Quinn slams hard into the side of the building, gripping his shoulder. He roars, then pulls his hand away. His palm is coated with blood but he ignores it. He returns fire, and the asshole who tagged him drops to the ground. Not missing a beat, Quinn presses forward.

Not far off, we hear an engine trying to turn over and spot a Viper behind the wheel of the van we saw parked outside Charley's days ago. I look at Quinn, then motion for him to cover the passenger side. I walk up on the asshole, yank open the driver's door, and press the barrel end of my gun to his temple. It's the Vipers' very own Prez. The motherfucker is abandoning his men. His eyes fall to his lap, where a gun lies. "Give me a reason to pull this trigger right now, motherfucker," I grind out, reach over and take his weapon, then step back. "Out," I order. The coward narrows his eyes at me as he slides from the seat of the van.

As fast as the battle began, all gunfire ceases. I detect movement out the corner of my eye, jerk my head to my right, and find myself staring down the barrel of a shotgun.

I made peace with death a long time ago.

Eyes wide open, I wait for the impact.

A gun fires.

The pain I expected never happens.

The bastard's weapon slips from his hands, and his body sways. He thuds to the frozen ground near my feet.

Quinn looks at me.

I don't speak.

Neither does he.

Never lowering his gun, Quinn swings around, his focus going behind him at the sound of footsteps to find Jake and the rest of the brothers marching toward us. "What do we have here?" Jake stops a few feet from where I stand. Grabbing the President by the back of his neck, I give him a shove.

"On your knees." I force him to the ground.

Jake looks down at the son of a bitch. "Looks like you're the last man standing."

The fucker spits on Jake's boot. "You'll pay for the massacre of my men. There are more of us. Word of our deaths will travel, and they will avenge me," he sneers.

Jake lifts his arm and presses the barrel end of his gun between the bastard's eyes, his eyes cold. "Then death waits for them too." He pulls the trigger.

"What should we do with the bodies?" I ask.

Jake looks at me. "Burn em'."


Almost an hour later, we are back on the road headed for the clubhouse. All evidence of today's events we left to burn inside the old logging mill. There's a strong possibility the Royal Viper's final warning is genuine—there could be more of them. If it's true, and the day comes they seek revenge... we'll be ready.

It's taking longer than usual to get back to our families. The snowstorm is hammering down on us, making road conditions worse by the minute. "I just checked online. They're starting to close roads down through town. Let's hope we don't run into any barricades trying to get to the clubhouse," Quinn says.

Logan's phone rings. "Hey, Angel," he greets his woman, Bella. "Whoa, slow down, babe." His tone gets my attention. I feel Logan's eyes on me, so I look at him. "Alba is in labor." My breath gets stuck in my throat. "They called for an ambulance, but road conditions are making response time longer than normal," Logan says. "Listen. We're twenty minutes away." My brother continues his conversation with Bella. "Hold up." He passes the phone toward me. "It's Alba."

I take the phone from him and place it to my ear. "Babe."

"I'm okay." Her words wash over me like she knew I needed to hear them. Alba moans then blows out a heavy breath.

"Contraction?"

"Yeah." She breathes through the pain. "Gabriel..." her voice drifts into a grunt, then it's Bella's voice I hear.

"Hello?"

"Take care of her," I tell Bella.

"We got this, big guy." The call ends, and I pass the phone back to Logan, who informs Jake what is happening at the clubhouse.


Luckily, we make it to the compound without running into road closures. I can't get out of the SUV fast enough after skidding to a stop. Leaving the keys in the ignition and the engine running, I rush toward the door, damn near taking it off its hinges when I burst inside the clubhouse. Mostly everyone we left behind is sitting downstairs with the children. The only ones missing: Bella, Emerson, Lisa, Mila, and my woman.

"They're upstairs," my sister says, holding Val.

Wasting no time, I take the stairs two at a time getting to Alba. I find her and the other women in our room. Bella is by her side, and Mila has a phone to her ear. "Gabriel," Alba says with an exhausted breath. "I'm not making it to the hospital."

"Alba, honey. The baby is crowning. I need you to bear down and push with the next contraction," Emerson states and I overhear Mila repeat what is happening on the phone, so 911 must be on the other end of the line.

"Ambulance is fifteen minutes away," Mila says.

"Fuck. This is happening." I look from Alba to Emerson.

Her eyes soften. "The baby is waiting for no one. Her contractions are on top of one another. I need you to focus on momma. Slide-in behind Alba and help brace her as she pushes."

I kick my dirty boots off my feet, then get on the bed behind my woman, placing her between my thighs. Alba presses her back into my chest. I brush her sweat-dampened hair from her face and kiss her temple. "You've got this, Mi Amor."

Alba grinds her teeth and wails as another contraction hits.

"Push, Alba," Emerson coaches.

I cage Alba in with my arms, giving her something to anchor herself, her hands wrap over my forearms, her nails digging into my flesh as she bears down.

"That's it," Emerson praises. "One more push, and the baby is out." Alba bears down again. Alba slumps against my chest, her head falling back as she catches her breath. I kiss her forehead and comfort her while I watch Mila pass a suction bulb to Emerson.

I hold my breath waiting for the sound all parents hope to hear.

The baby's cries fill the room.

Emerson places our baby girl on Alba's chest. "Skin to skin, momma, so we can keep the baby warm."

I'm speechless as, inside of me, emotions overflow. My woman brought another life into this world. Another tiny version of our love.

Within a few moments, the room floods with men in EMT uniforms. The entire time my focus is on my newborn and my wife. Everything else fades into the background until Bella walks back into the bedroom with Gabe and my sister, holding Val.

Our sisters bring the children to the side of the bed, seeing us before Alba and the baby can be loaded onto a stretcher and taken to the hospital. I look past people moving about the small space and notice several faces trying to catch a glimpse of the newest family member from the hallway.

I'm warmed and overwhelmed by the amount of love in the room and from my family watching. I kiss Alba's temple again and place my hand over hers that's resting on the baby. "You did good, Momma."

"Isn't she perfect?" Alba whispers, keeping this moment private and to ourselves.

I swallow the lump of emotion clogging my throat. "She is," I agree. "Thank you for such a wonderful gift."

**10**

———

**ALBA**

It's been three days since I gave birth to Catalina at the clubhouse. What a wild experience that was, but I wouldn't change a minute of it for anything in the world. Whereas Gabe and Val take after their father, Catalina looks like me with her pale blonde hair and big blue eyes. The doctors kept us in the hospital for two days, and finally, we are back home. And I was more than ready, although Gabriel was more prepared than me. While he stayed with the baby and me at the hospital, Gabe and Val stayed with my sister and Logan, and Gabriel doesn't do well when he doesn't have his family together under one roof with him. He gets restless. Gabriel is not one of those parents that looks forward to the kids staying the night with family so Mom and Dad can have a break. No, my husband is the opposite.

"Mommy." I hear my son call for me, and I'm pulled from my wandering thoughts. Sitting up in bed, I look at Gabe, who is standing at the foot of my bed with his sister. Both are still in their pajamas and have serious bed heads.

"Good morning," I chirp. "Climb up here and give me some love."

Gabe and Val jump up onto the bed and laugh when I start peppering kisses all over their faces.

"Can we open presents now?" Gabe asks.

"Yay!" Val claps her hands.

I ruffle Gabe's hair. "How about I go find Papi, and we eat breakfast before we open presents."

Gabe and Val nod.

"Now, you two brush your teeth, then go downstairs. I'll be down in a minute." Since I went into labor on Christmas Eve and spent a couple of days in the hospital, Gabe and Val didn't get to open our presents on Christmas day. They weren't too disappointed since Bella and Logan bought just as much for my kids as they did theirs, so the kids still had a fantastic Christmas morning with their aunt, uncle, and cousins.

Hopping down from the bed, the kids rush out of the room. A few seconds later, I go in search of my husband, and I know exactly where to find him. When I come upon the nursery, I faintly hear Gabriel speaking to the baby in Spanish, and when I push open the door, I find him sitting in the rocking chair with our daughter lying across his bare chest. The sight before me takes my breath away.

"Hey," I call out, keeping my voice low.

Gabriel lifts his eyes to mine and rewards me with one of his rare smiles. The kind of smile that makes his whole face light up.

Walking up behind the chair, I drape my arms over Gabriel's shoulders, press my face against his cheek, and breathe in his scent. "How long have you been up?"

I get a grunt in response. That's Gabriel's way of saying *a while*. He was like this when we first brought Gabe and Val home from the hospital, too. He spent weeks barely getting any sleep because he'd spend hours watching over them at night or just holding them. Running my finger through his hair, I kiss his neck. "The kids want to open presents. Do you want to put Cat in her crib or bring her down with us?" I ask.

"I'll bring her."

When Gabriel and I walk into the living room, Gabe and Val are nosing around the Christmas tree. Gabriel places the baby in the bassinet beside the sofa then walks over to Gabe and Val. Leaning down, he scoops them into his arms. "Feliz Navidad," he rumbles.

"Merry Christmas, Papi," Gabe says while Val tugs at Gabriel's beard and babbles her own version of Merry Christmas.

"What do you two think we should do first? Eat breakfast or open presents?" Gabriel asks the kids.

"Presents!" they shout in unison.

Over the next thirty minutes, we watch Gabe and Val tear into their gifts. Gabe just about lost his mind when Gabriel went outside and returned with a mini street bike for him. Gabriel and I went rounds about whether to get our son a motorcycle because, in my eyes, he's just a baby, and I don't want him to get hurt. But at the end of the day, I relented because I knew Gabriel would never let anything happen to his son. Also, Gabe is just like his father, and right now he's currently paying rapt attention to his father as he gives him instruction on how to handle the bike.

"Gabe," I call out. My son looks at me. "Do you want to give Papi his present?"

Gabe looks at his father, then back to me, and nods. Abandoning his bike, he makes his way over to the tree and picks up the one small box that's left. Making his way back over to Gabriel, he hands over the box with a proud look on his face.

"Gabe has been saving his allowance and even picked that out by himself," I supply. I tried to help pay for the gift, but my little boy insisted he do it himself.

I can't help but smile as I watch Gabriel tear at the wrapping paper and then watch as a look I have never seen before washes over his face. Flipping the pocket watch over, Gabriel reads the inscription on the back and visibly swallows.

*A son's first hero is his dad.*

The inscription is something Gabriel said to Gabe one day when our son asked about his grandfather. Gabriel often shares some of the happy memories of his father, and one of those was when his father had given him a pocket watch when he was a teenager. The watch was passed down through several generations. Unfortunately, Gabriel lost it during a time when he was homeless. Some junkie had robbed him, stealing the timepiece.

Fisting the watch in one hand, Gabriel grips the back of Gabe's neck with the other, then brings Gabe's forehead to his. Something monumental passes between father and son, and I don't dare say a word to interrupt. "Best gift I've ever gotten, *hijo.*" Gabriel's voice comes out gruff.

Later that night, after the kids have gone to bed, Gabriel and I sit on the sofa, with me on his lap. A fire crackles in the fireplace. The glow of the tree's lights paints the living room wall, and my eyes stay fixed on watching the snowfall through the large picture window.

"I love you, Gabriel," I murmur, snuggling deeper into his embrace.

"I love you more, Cariño."